More titles in this series:

Walter and Willy Go to the City
Walter and Willy in Outer Space

Copyright © 2023 Clavis Publishing Inc., New York

Visit us on the Web at www.clavis-publishing.com.

Walter and Willy Go Fishing written by Bonnie Grubman and illustrated by Judi Abbot

ISBN 978-1-60537-688-2

This book was printed in February 2023 at Nikara, M. R. Štefánika 858/25, 963 01 Krupina, Slovakia.

First Edition
10 9 8 7 6 5 4 3 2 1

Walter and Willy Go Fishing

Clavis

NEW YORK

Written by Bonnie Grubman
Illustrated by Judi Abbot

While **Willy** scanned the water,
Walter rummaged through the tackle box.

"Shhh," said Willy. "You'll scare the fish away."

"Me? What about you? That neon vest screams 'scram' to the fish!"

"But I like my vest . . ."

"I'm sorry," Walter said.
"I'm just trying to help you . . .

. . . catch a really **big** fish."

"Like I need help from you,"
Willy said, making his first cast.
"Just watch."
They waited for a bite . . .
and waited,
and waited.

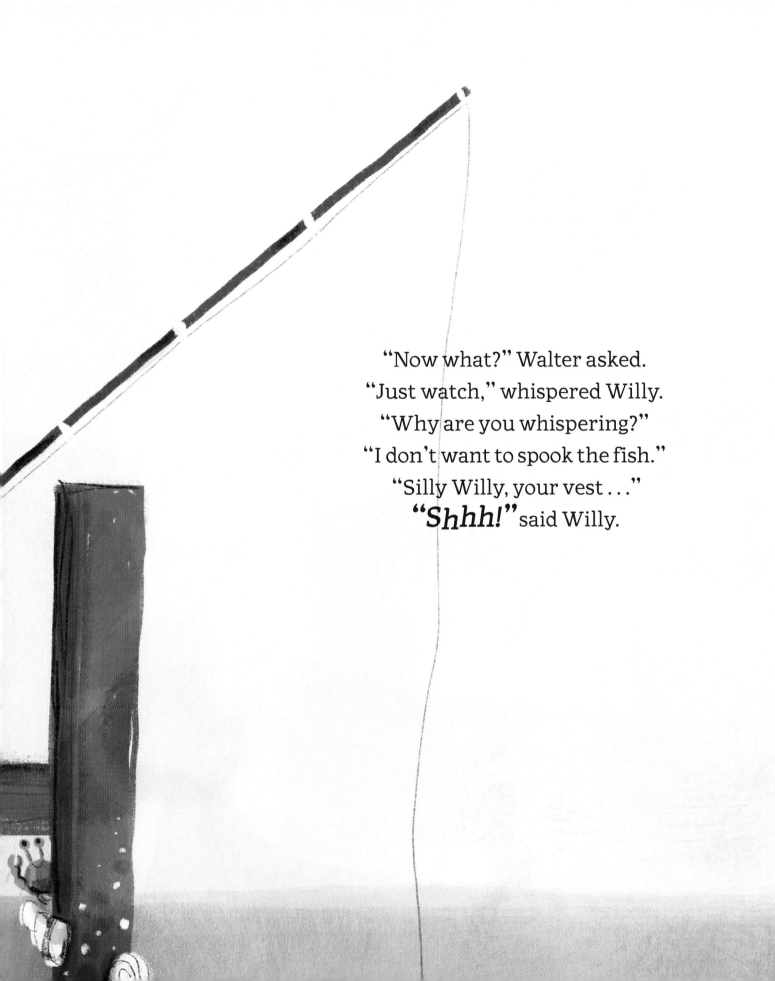

"Now what?" Walter asked.
"Just watch," whispered Willy.
"Why are you whispering?"
"I don't want to spook the fish."
"Silly Willy, your vest . . ."
"Shhh!" said Willy.

"You don't even like fish," Walter muttered.
"I know," Willy replied. "But I like fishing."
"Why?"
"Because it's relaxing."
"You don't look relaxed," Walter said.
He leaned back and gazed at the sky.
"*This* is how you relax."

After a quick nap, Walter opened his eyes.
"Any nibbles yet, Willy?"
"Just from mosquitoes," Willy said.
"Mosquitoes!" Walter yelled.
"Let's move to another spot."

Willy shrugged. "I like it here just fine.
Anyway, you know nothing about fishing, Walter.
Try learning more and talking less."

Okay, I will, thought Walter.
He grabbed a fishing guidebook
and read it from cover to cover.

"*Psst* . . . Willy," murmured Walter.
"Don't bother whispering anymore,"
Willy said. "I've tried everything."
"Except taking off your vest."
Walter pointed at the book.
"Look **here.** See?"

"Don't believe everything you read," Willy humphed.

"Even the part about whispering?" Walter asked.

SPLA

Willy jumped into the water and cast his line as far as he could.
Then he waited, and waited, and waited.

"How's it going out there, Willy?" Walter called.
Willy sighed. **"Just be patient."**

Poor stubborn Willy, thought Walter.
But then he had an idea. "Willy!" he shouted.
"Could we *please* move to the shade?
The sun is **burning** my snout."

"Fine!" Willy shouted back.
"But I won't take off my vest."

Walter settled in the shade
while Willy cast his line from the shore.
Then they waited,
and waited,
and waited.
Until Walter had another idea.
"Willy!" he shouted. **"What's that smell?"**

Willy sniffed.
Then Walter shouted:
"You smell like roasted pig!"

"Ewww!" Willy ripped off his vest.
"Maybe it's hotter than I thought . . ."

"Come on, there's a pond close-by
where it's much cooler," Walter said.
And hopefully full of fish, he thought.

At the pond, Willy cast his line into the still water.
"Mmm, smell that fresh air," said Walter.
"It's so quiet here. Listen!"
"You too, Walter."

So they listened to the loons and
the croaking frogs. Soon they spotted
turtles basking on a log and watched
a mother duck preen her flock of ducklings.
"Isn't this nice, Walter?"
"The only way to fish, Willy."

And suddenly . . . the line twitched.
It tugged and jerked.
Willy sprang to his feet,
tightened his grip on the rod,
pulled it upwards, and **HOP!**

"Now that's how you catch a fish," cheered Willy.

"It sure is," said Walter.

They went hog wild (of course).
Then Willy gently released the fish back into the pond.
"Goodbye, little fishy," he said and thought,
you're a real catch too, Walter.